Onyx Kids

Shiloh's School Dayz

Book One

The Sealed Locker

By Rita Onyx

Onyx Star Publishing, LLC
Delaware, USA

To every kid who decided to read instead
of watching a screen,
actually, you're probably reading this on a
phone so thank you for just choosing to
read

Table of Contents

Chapter 1
It's a dog-eat-dog world

8:00 am to 9:00 am

"Hey, Shiloh, wait up!" said Evan. It was the first day of school at Cornerstone Middle School and both boys were a little late so they were rushing.

"Which homeroom are you in?" Shiloh asked as soon as Evan caught up to him.

"I'm in, uh, let's see…Mr. Thomas's class," said Evan as he tried to read the crumpled paper he had in his hand. He was a little out of breath from running to catch up to Shiloh and didn't realize he almost ruined his schedule. He was weighed down by his backpack which was loaded up with his iPad and Apple Pencil which together didn't weigh much, but he also had a bunch of his futuristic gadgets that he had been working on over the summer. Evan's main goal in life was to be a mix of Doc from *Back To The Future* and Q from *James Bond*.

"I'm in Ms. Sufferin's class," said Shiloh. "Aw man, I was hoping we'd be in the same homeroom so I wouldn't have to suffer alone."

Evan immediately stopped and looked around. "Hey! Be careful, she's always lurking around and if she catches you saying that she'll be on you faster than a fly swatter on a fly."

"Looks like we're good. I don't see–

All of a sudden, they were face to face with Ms. Sufferin and her huge glasses that made her beady eyes look enormous. Her permanent scowl was firmly in place which seemed impossible since her bun

6

was so tight it looked like it was going to pull the skin off of her face.

"A-ha! I caught you two little–

Ms. Sufferin did hear them, but fortunately for Shiloh and Evan at that same moment Mr. Thomas walked by and stopped to say hello. Immediately Ms. Sufferin replaced her scowl with a smile, or what could almost pass for one if she were capable of joy.

"Mr. Thomas! I didn't see you. I was just reminding these two little rascals to go to class." Ms. Sufferin said as she straightened her already slick hair and drab outfit.

Shiloh started to wonder if Ms. Sufferin had a crush on Mr. Thomas. He thought of them together for a second since they were both single, but he didn't want to do that to Mr. Thomas, not even in his imagination.

"Hi Shiloh and Evan. I'm happy to see you guys. When you and your parents came for new student orientation I was glad to meet you all. We're going to have a wonderful school year," Mr. Thomas said with a smile. "I'll see you in class Evan." He walked off and left them with Ms. Sufferin in the hall.

Ms. Sufferin continued to paste what she thought was a smile on her face until Mr. Thomas walked into his class. Since Ms. Sufferin was distracted Shiloh and Evan made a run for it down the hall in order to get to class on time.

Don't worry, we'll catch up between classes and at lunch," said Evan as they raced into class. "Have a good one."

Shiloh and Evan had been friends since Shiloh's family had moved into the house next door to Evan's in fourth grade. Evan had invited Shiloh over and showed him his cool gadgets. Shiloh had never seen a kid's room like Evan's. Evan's dad and mom were both scientists and their interests had spilled over into Evan. His room looked more like a mysterious laboratory than a bedroom. There were wires and the insides of old computers strewn everywhere. He had lit neon signs that said things like "What Is Now Proved Was Once Only Imagined" and bobbleheads of Albert Einstein and Isaac Newton. There wasn't a trace of sports stuff unless you counted his bucket of contraptions that tried to make you run faster or hit harder.

Shiloh slid into a chair at the back of the room and set his backpack down. He'd been looking forward to starting middle school, but he missed the old familiar surroundings of his elementary class and his fifth-grade teacher, Mrs. Hudson. She was friendly and soft-spoken and the complete opposite of Ms. Sufferin. She was a natural born teacher who loved kids in contrast to Ms. Sufferin who acted like she hated kids. Even when Mrs. Hudson had to scold you, she did it in a quiet way and always made you understand it was for your own good. Ms. Sufferin on the other hand seemed to make a hobby of scolding.

All you had to do is take one look at Ms. Sufferin's classroom to know that this was her domain. There were steel chairs and desks and no bulletin boards with fun art. There were some new computers set up along one side of the room, but no decorations anywhere. There wasn't even a "Welcome New Students" sign. The room looked decidedly stark. Shiloh wasn't sure if that was because it was the first day and Ms. Sufferin hadn't had time to decorate yet or if she was just not into decorating. It was probably the latter.

A few minutes before the bell rang for homeroom to begin, Ms. Sufferin walked in. She was pencil thin with a long face, bushy eyebrows and no makeup. She wore huge round-rimmed glasses and had her hair pulled back in the tightest bun possible. She was dressed in a plain white shirt with a white collar, plain long black skirt, black stockings, and black Mary Janes. Altogether, her looks and outfit made her hopelessly out of fashion and weirdly like Olive Oyl from *Popeye*.

The students in class were muttering quietly under their breaths, which was fortunate because it seemed like Ms. Sufferin's one gift might be the hearing of a dog or even a bat. Ms. Sufferin stood in front of the class surveying her class from end to end.

"Hmmph," She grunted.

Turning sharply on her heels she wrote her name on the whiteboard. She underlined "Ms." three times so Shiloh took that to mean that she didn't want to be called "Mrs." by mistake.

"Morning class," said Ms. Sufferin as she stood behind the shiny steel desk.

"Good morning," the class said in unison.

Ms. Sufferin slammed her hand down on the desk. "I didn't say 'Good Morning'! I'll be the judge on whether this morning is good. You're all in middle school now, so I hope you're ready for things to be vastly different than they were in elementary school. This is a place of L-E-A-R-N-I-N-G. For those who can't spell that means learning. It's not a place for snapchatting, texting, or any other socializing. This isn't a fashion show so this is also not the place for announcing what you are wearing or caring about what other kids wear. This is why, if I get my way, uniforms will be instituted by next year! If only they would listen to me!!" She put up both of her hands in frustration and looked up at the ceiling. It was almost as if she forgot that she wasn't alone.

 She abruptly put her hands down and looked back down at the class, daring anyone to say anything about her mini breakdown with a hard stare. She then continued, "It's time to get serious about your studies if you ever expect to make it into a good high school and college. It's never too early to start."

Kids were squirming in their chairs, but nobody said a word. Ms. Sufferin continued, "It's a dog-eat-dog world out there so if you want to survive you better apply yourself." She then growled and barked and started to chomp on imaginary food to emphasize her point.

Shiloh had kept a straight face up until this point, but this was too much and he started to softly snicker. He could take the words, but the barking and chomping was over the top. As soon as the laugh came out of his mouth he knew that he was in big trouble.

Right away Ms. Sufferin with her superhero hearing pointed at him with her long finger. "You there, young man, who *ARE* you? Stand up and give me your name!"

Shiloh stood up slowly next to his desk. "My name's Shiloh, ma'am...I mean Mrs., no I mean Ms. Sufferin." Her eyes bugged out and her eyebrows shot up at 'Mrs.,' which could only mean that Shiloh had just made the situation even worse.

"Do you think what I'm saying is funny, Shiloh?" she demanded.

"Yes...I mean, no, Ms. Sufferin. Learning is serious and I don't take it lightly," said Shiloh as he tried to show that he was listening.

Shiloh glanced at Ms. Sufferin's face for a brief second and then looked sideways and down as if he were shielding his eyes from harsh sunlight. There was a girl seated next to him on the left that he hadn't noticed before. He thought he saw her lips curling into a smile, but she was keeping her head still so he wasn't sure.

"I can see I'm going to have to make some changes in this seating arrangement. All troublemakers are up front with me so I can keep an eye on them," said Ms. Sufferin. She furiously began erasing and writing then leaned back to admire her handiwork.

"Yes, this will work. This will work perfectly," she said with a sneer. "Don't just sit there! Pass this back." Ms. Sufferin handed the updated seating chart to the person in the front row. As the students learned where their new seats were, you could hear the hum of low-level groans slowly spreading among the students. No one liked seating charts.

"When you figure out where you're sitting permanently, then just get up quietly, and I mean quietly, and move to that chair." said Ms. Sufferin with authority.

Shiloh let out an exasperated air of frustration when he saw the seating chart. Originally, Ms. Sufferin had had him sitting at the very back of the room close to where he was, which would have been perfect, but now he had been assigned to a chair up front, right across from Ms. Sufferin's desk. As he made his way to the front the girl he had noticed before smiled at him and passed him a small folded-up note. Shiloh was careful not to draw any attention to himself as he put the note into his pocket.

"I said QUIETLY!" Ms. Sufferin yelled. She looked very annoyed with the amount of noise they were making as they moved from chair to chair. Of course, most of the noise was coming from the slamming around of backpacks although some of the guys were deliberately making noise to show their protest of the seating chart.

It was as if Ms. Sufferin had a sixth sense because she had somehow managed to figure out how to position all the students in the class so they weren't near their friends. How she had done this without knowing the students yet was a complete mystery.

Shiloh was frustrated with himself for laughing. He could have had a chair in the back out of harm's way, but now he was in the spotlight under Ms. Sufferin's watchful eye. He was also in danger of being struck by the ridiculously long pointer that Ms. Sufferin twirled around as if it were a baton. As soon as they sat down and all the backpacks had been moved into appropriate positions, a heavy, cold silence fell upon the class. Ms. Sufferin stood up and began to explain their schedules to them as if they were coordinating a cross-country move.

"This is homeroom. Here is where you all are lucky enough to start your day with me!" Ms. Sufferin said with an impossibly deep scowl as she peered around the classroom daring anyone to scoff at her choice of the word "lucky".

"After homeroom, you have to go and bother another teacher and then another one and so on. I have given you a packet that you should open to find out your locker and a map of the school. Maybe you all will surprise me and actually follow directions, although I doubt it," she said with disdain.

In elementary school, Shiloh had stayed in one classroom for most of the day, but middle school was different. As he looked at the school map and where his classes were held, he realized that it was going to take a lot of sprinting to get from class to class in time.

How am I going to remember all of this? Shiloh thought. He was beginning to worry that he wouldn't remember which class he was supposed to go to and when!

The hour-long homeroom period seemed to stretch into three hours as Ms. Sufferin was attempting to give them valuable information about their new life at Cornerstone, but Shiloh didn't hear most of it. He was busy thinking about how he was going to set reminders in his phone so it would send him notifications to remind him which class to go to, where he was supposed to go, and when to go.

Shiloh had just gotten his new cell phone a few weeks before and he was still learning how to use it. His parents had debated whether or not to buy it for him, but when Evan told him that 83% of all middle-school kids already had them, Shiloh had used that data to convince his parents. His parents were tech people so it wasn't that hard to convince them that it was in their best interest to be able to call or text him if there was an emergency.

[[[RING]]] Finally, finally, finally, the bell rang to move on to the next class and for Ms. Sufferin to stop her endless droning. It looked like Ms. Sufferin was just as happy for the bell because she stopped talking abruptly and licked her fingers to straighten her eyebrows. She dashed out of the room without even a glance back. Probably to go and see Mr. Thomas Shiloh figured.

There was a 10-minute change before the start of the next session and the students had been directed to dump off their stuff in their assigned lockers before going to the next class. Now that computers and iPads had replaced most of the books Shiloh didn't feel that he needed a locker. Having lockers was a throwback to his parents' days, but since he wanted to follow the rules he decided to drop by his locker anyway to at least know where it was, just in case.

Shiloh opened up the orientation packet that Ms. Sufferin had given them. Each packet had their weekly schedule, a campus map, and information about how to get into their lockers including their unique combination, which they had been asked to keep in a safe place.

Shiloh found his locker quickly and he saw that Evan's locker was only about 5 lockers away from his. The girl from class bounced in to open up her locker too. Hers was in between Evan's and Shiloh's. She smiled in Shiloh's direction and after she crammed all her stuff into her locker, she wandered over.

Out of the corner of his eye, Shiloh noticed that Evan was staring at her. *Oh no, not again*, Shiloh thought. Evan always started crushing on a girl on the first day of school. Shiloh had told him to not get caught up so quickly but he wouldn't listen. Evan was always convinced that she was the one...for the school year at least.

"Hi, I'm Desirae." Desirae said to Shiloh. She was a little shorter than he was and standing a little too close. "Did you open my note?"

He took a step back to get some space. Shiloh had completely forgotten about the note. "Not yet. I was afraid to with Sufferin staring at me non-stop. Thought she might bop me with that pointer."

"I think you would've survived," said Desirae as she laughed flirtatiously. She stopped abruptly and had a funny look on her face. "Hey, I wonder why that locker next to yours is taped up?" she asked curiously.

Shiloh was so concentrated on opening up his locker that he hadn't noticed a huge padlock on the locker to the right of his. Not only was it locked down tight, there was fire-engine-red tape making a huge "X" across the front of the locker. The tape had the words "danger do not enter" and "peligro no entrar."

By this time, Evan had come up to both of them.

"Hi," said Evan shyly at Desirae.

"Hi," she said back shortly, trying to sound as disinterested as possible.

Of course, this was all lost on Evan who turned to Shiloh and gave him a nod up as if to confirm that Desirae was as interested as he was. Shiloh could only shake his head.

"I wonder why that locker is taped up," Evan said.

"Yeah, Shiloh and I were wondering the same thing." Desirae mused. "*Do Not Enter* Hmm...if this is so dangerous then why even have this here? Why not just remove this locker?" She fiddled with the lock.

Evan cleared his throat and elbowed Shiloh in his ribs a little too sharply. He made a sharp groan and gave Evan a hard look.

"Do you two know each other?" asked Shiloh, trying to sound casual.

"Not officially," said Evan, "aren't you Desirae? You won the science competition last year with your handheld earthquake detector, didn't you?"

"Yeah, I did," said Desirae. "I can't believe you remembered that." Her lack of interest suddenly doing a 180.

For a few minutes, the three of them had forgotten about the mysterious locker and laughed and talked about school and what they did for the summer. There was an easy comradery that was developing among the three of them. Shiloh thought that maybe this year was going to be uneventful and he almost relaxed.

But before he could, something happened that brought it right back to the forefront of their minds.

Chapter 2
I hate roaches!

9:00 am to 10:00 am

It was almost time for their next period, although much to Evan's annoyance he and Desirae weren't in the same class. They were just about to turn away from the mysterious locker when one of the janitors walked by.

"Excuse me," said Evan. "Can you tell us what's going on here? Why is this locker boarded up?"

The janitor had been pushing a large rolling bucket with a mop. He had on dark grey overalls with the name "Tom" stitched on them. He was middle-aged with grey streaks through his dark hair, but strangely enough his hands looked more like a business executive's instead of a worker's. He had sneaky looking eyes that eyed the kids up and down. He was startled by Evan's inquiry and for a second he didn't say anything. "Stay away from it," he said gruffly. "You don't need to know. It's absolutely none of your business...unless you got a dollar on you."

Evan and his friends were taken aback by the blatant money grab. "What do you need a dollar for?" Evan asked.

"These haircuts don't pay for themselves," Tom said in a thick Brooklyn accent. He took out a small black comb and ran it through his slicked back hair.

Before they could answer him, a sudden movement caught their eye. A small moving object crawled out of the slit

23

under the locker door. Shiloh, Evan, and Desirae couldn't see exactly what it was before the janitor grabbed the object with one swift move. He took a matchbox out of his left back pocket and put the twitching object inside.

"What was that?" asked Desirae.

"Uh, never mind what that was. Like I said before, you don't need to know what that was," Tom said as he looked around paranoid.

"I have a dollar!" Shiloh exclaimed, waving it in the air.

"The price just went up!" Tom spat. He quickly gathered the mop and bucket and quickly rolled away.

"Then what's the price?" Evan called behind him.

"You can't afford it!" Tom shouted back before disappearing around the corner.

They watched him until he was gone before they resumed their conversation.

"From what I saw I thought whatever it was moved like a roach," said Evan.

"Ew, I hate roaches," said Desirae as she batted away imaginary roaches from her arms. "If roaches are in that locker I don't want to touch it, in fact I don't even want to be near it."

"Why would a janitor keep a roach in a matchbox instead of killing it?" said Shiloh.

"I don't know," said Evan, "but I think we should find out."

"We're late for class. Catch you both later," said Shiloh. In his rush to stash his stuff in his locker, he accidentally took out his math book instead of his English book. *Arrgghhh,* he thought to himself, but it was too late to open his locker again now because he had to get to class. The only seats left were in the front, so he took the seat closest to the door and started to plan how he was going to escape with a quick bathroom break so he could get his English book.

Luckily, Mr. Thomas, Evan's homeroom teacher, was the instructor for Shiloh's English class. He was the polar opposite of Ms. Sufferin. While she was cold and strict, he was friendly and casual. Ms. Sufferin thought that school was torture, but Mr. Thomas thought that learning should be fun.

He introduced himself and told the students how he was also a writer and was working on an epic sci-fi novel. As he talked, his excitement over his new book seemed to be coming out of his blue eyes like electricity. Shiloh had never even thought about becoming a writer. Sure, he liked to read and had always gotten "A's" in English class, but listening to Mr. Thomas speak was making him think about new things. He decided then and there to try to be a star in Mr. Thomas's class.

But, in order to be a star, he definitely needed his textbook. He mentioned that he had grabbed the wrong book and Mr. Thomas gave him a hall pass without any fuss. Shiloh was so glad that he was nothing like Ms. Sufferin. If it was her she would have made an example out of him the whole class period.

Shiloh quickly ran down the hallway to open up his locker at the same time he started to rummage through his pockets. *Oh no!* He thought as he realized he had locked his orientation packet inside his locker! The packet had the sheet of paper with the school map and his lock combination. He should have written it on one of his hands like the other kids had done.

He went through his pockets again and found a short pencil and felt a piece of paper folded around it. That's when he remembered Desirae's folded note. He took it out, and opened it to see a funny sketch of a big dog with huge open jaws running after a tiny dog. There weren't any words.

For a second, he didn't get it.

Then, he remembered the "dog-eat-dog" incident and he laughed. Desirae was actually pretty smart and funny, and maybe a little cute...maybe. He shook his head as if to shake the thought out of his mind. That was Evan's crush and he was not going to get in the way of that...it's just that now he could kinda see why Evan liked her.

Ugh...I gotta stop thinking like that. I have to think about more important stuff right now, like how am I going to get into my locker? Hmmm....how would Evan solve this? Shiloh had so many thoughts running through his head.

Ok, first I'm going to write down what I remember.

He flipped the note over and wrote down: 3-5-7. He remembered that there was a "9" and also a "1" but he wasn't sure what the other number was and he wasn't sure what order the numbers were in.

He looked at the lock and saw that he had left the dial closer to "1" than to "9" so he was guessing that it was either some number, 9, and then 1 or 9, then some number, then 1. He felt like 9 and 1 sandwiching in the other number was probably right. Luckily, there were only five other numbers to pick from 0, 2, 4, 6, or 8. He was pretty sure he would have remembered either 0 or 2, so he tried 3-5-7-9-4-1 first, but that didn't work. Next, he tried 3-5-7-9-6-1 and that thankfully worked.

Once he got it, he took Desirae's note and figured out what the numbers would be if letters of the alphabet were assigned to them: C-E-G-I-F-A. He had remembered Evan saying once that letters were much easier for most people to remember than numbers. He wrote his "code word" on the side with the dog art.

Right before he swung open the door to his locker, he saw something that stopped him in his tracks. It was another roach climbing toward the sealed-up locker as if it were in a trance. Shiloh began to imagine his gym clothes and backpack being infested and it wasn't a pleasant thought. He took his stuff out and shook it frantically, but there weren't any roaches. He breathed a sigh of relief, but he decided to take his stuff out just to be sure.

He crammed everything into his backpack, and headed out. He wasn't going to put his stuff back in there until the mystery of the locker was solved. If he brought roaches home in his stuff, his mom was going to be extremely upset. She had a severe bug phobia and screamed even when she saw the tiniest ant.

Down the hall, Tom was mopping up a section of the floor. He looked up and gave Shiloh an odd look. *Didn't he clean that hallway before?* Shiloh thought. He wondered why Tom was still hanging around that same spot.

"Whaddya lookin' at kid? Can't you see I'm workin' here?" Tom said as he literally mopped the same spot over and over again.

Shiloh raced back to class and slid into his seat. He was so glad that Mr. Thomas was his English teacher and not Ms. Sufferin. Mr. Thomas was bringing around a glass jar with slips of paper in it that had topics written on them. Each student was supposed to pick one out of the jar. As soon as all the students had picked a topic, Mr. Thomas began to explain the assignment.

"Class, please turn to page 25 in your textbook and read the instructions on how to write a persuasive argument," he said. "Now open up the slip of paper you selected to see what your topic is. Everyone has different topics. I want you to write a one page essay on your side of the argument."

Shiloh opened up the slip to see: *Summer break - Should they be so long?*

Easy, that's a big YES. In fact, they should be longer! Shiloh thought to himself. *Now how am I going to make "yes" into an essay?*

"Does anyone have any questions?" Mr. Thomas asked. "Please tell me your name when I call on you. I should have your names down in one or two more classes."

"Mr. Thomas, my name is Rose. How are we supposed to write a whole page?" She asked. "I could answer my question with one word."

The whole class nodded in agreement.

"That's a good question, Rose. I'd like you back up your arguments with facts and figures and more importantly elaborate on your thoughts. I am very interested to hear your opinions."

Shiloh raised his hand.

"Yes, Shiloh, what's your question?" Mr. Thomas asked.

"You mean, this isn't only about our opinion? Shiloh asked.

"Another good question. I want to hear your opinions but keep in mind that no matter what side you choose you have to back it up with facts that support it," said Mr. Thomas, "Think about which side you're most passionate about. You're allowed to use the internet for research. If you don't have your iPads and the computers in the back are taken, I will give you a 15-minute hall pass for the library to use their computers. Just make sure you're on research sites and not on *Roblox*! Besides, it's blocked anyways!"

The class laughed knowing that was exactly what they would do if they had a chance.

Mr. Thomas continued, "You can even interview me or any of the other teachers for their opinions if you like.

Shiloh thought about what it would be like to interview Ms. Sufferin. She'd probably say that there shouldn't be any summer break at all. In fact, she would say there shouldn't be weekends off either. Which was so weird to Shiloh because she hated teaching so why she wanted to spend more time in the classroom stumped him. Just the thought of her scrunched up face with her huge glasses and piercing eyes gave him the shivers.

"Just remember that opinions are different than facts. That's very important! You'll have two class periods and time at home to work on this project." Mr. Thomas reminded them.

There were eight computers in the class so students had to work together to get their research finished. No one had gotten out of their assigned seats yet.

Mr. Thomas encouraged them to get moving. "Unless you all have somehow managed to tap into the internet using your mind I don't understand why everyone is not in front of an iPad or computer." At once everyone started to get up and get their iPads or get to the back to where the computers were.

Shiloh immediately got up and walked to one of the computers, but another student got there at the same time.

"Hey, I'm Shiloh," he said to the other student.

"Yeah, I got that when you asked Mr. Thomas that question. My name's Max," the other student said.

"What's your topic?" Shiloh asked.

"Whether we should colonize Mars or not. What's yours?" Max asked though he didn't look at Shiloh and seemed somewhat disinterested. He was trying to sign into Roblox instead of researching his topic.

Just then, Mr. Thomas walked up behind them. "What's your name, son?" he asked Max.

"My name's Max, sir," Max replied a little too loudly with a slight sneer in his voice.

"Max, didn't you hear me when I said Roblox would be blocked?" Mr. Thomas asked.

"Sorry, I uh, accidentally typed in Roblox. It's like my brain is on autopilot ya know?"

Shiloh raised his eyebrows at this exchange. Max had a lot of guts being so blunt with the teacher. Mr. Thomas must have thought so too because his face looked very skeptical of what Max had just said.

"What site were you actually going to go on?" Mr. Thomas asked.

"Amazon," Max replied.

"What? Why?" Mr. Thomas was confused.

"For a book...it's called *The Case for Mars, Why We Should Settle There*," said Max, "I thought I could find a Kindle version for my iPad."

"Okay, just remember Amazon starts with an A and not an R," said Mr. Thomas. Shiloh could tell by the look on his face that Mr. Thomas didn't believe what Max was telling him.

As soon as Mr. Thomas was on the other side of the room, Shiloh asked, "How'd you know about that book?"

"Ha ha!" Max laughed under his breath. "My dad wrote it. I've got a gazillion copies of it at home."

Shiloh smiled. He liked something about Max, but he was certain that his parents wouldn't like him at all. "Whoa! What a coincidence...I mean that you would get that particular topic. And, it's cool that your dad's a writer like Mr. Thomas."

"No, it isn't a coincidence," said Max. "The girl next to me chose it and I read it over her shoulder while she was opening it. I gave her five bucks to switch with me since I didn't want to write about whether we should have a three-party political system or not. B-O-R-I-N-G. She doesn't like science and she was happy to have the money for the vending machine. And as far as my dad goes, he hasn't made a dime from his writing. He's always stuck

35

behind closed doors in his office pounding on the keyboard at night. He's an aerospace engineer otherwise we'd be living on the streets."

"Aren't you worried about getting in trouble if Mr. Thomas finds out you tricked him?" asked Shiloh.

"Naw," said Max. "I'm always in trouble anyway. Besides I'm going to write my own paper with a little help from *The Case for Mars.*"

Shiloh was going to say something else, but a text came in from Evan.

```
    Meet me at mysterious
locker at recess.
```

Shiloh texted back.

```
    I'll be there. Second
    roach spotted. Maybe
    something dead inside
    locker?
```

Evan sent another message.

```
    Don't think so. Didn't
    smell anything. Sent
    Desirae a note. She's
    meeting us. She's
    bringing a roach trap.
```

Shiloh texted again.

      `Remind me to tell you`
`about C-E-G-I-F-A.`

Chapter 3
Evan's secret lab

10:00 am to 11:00 am

"What's C-E-G-I-F-A?" Evan asked as soon as he and Shiloh met at his locker during their unfairly short, 20-minute recess period.

"Well, remember when you told me there's evidence that people can remember sequenced letters better than numbers?" asked Shiloh.

"Yeah, that's why some combination locks have letters now," said Evan. "People can create a word or use an unusual word and it's easy for them to remember, but hard for anyone else to crack." Shiloh was always amazed at how much knowledge Evan seemed to have about virtually every topic.

"I forgot part of my lock combination, but once I reasoned backwards and figured it out, I came up with C-E-G-I-F-A so I could remember it from now on," said Shiloh.

"That's catchy," said Evan, "but you shouldn't have told me because it's easy to remember and now I can break into your locker."

Shiloh looked shocked and then panicked.

"Ha, you should see your face!" Evan laughed and pointed. "I'm just kidding. I already forgot about it...or did I?" He kept on laughing.

"Well, joke's on you. There's nothing in there now but space anyway. I took out all my stuff. I wish we could figure out what's in that boarded-up locker," said Shiloh trying to change the subject. "If I get any roaches in my clothes, my mom is going to make me throw out my whole closet."

"I remember that time I was at your house and your mom went wild when she heard a cricket chirping inside." Evan said as he grinned.

"Yeah, after you left, my dad had to tear apart the entire house to find that cricket. He scooped it up with a glass and a piece of cardboard and put it outside," said Shiloh. "I wish we could've kept it. I would put it in Ms. Sufferin's desk and watch her jump." They both laughed at the thought.

Just then Desirae bounded up and wedged herself between the two friends. "Did you guys figure out what's in the locker yet? Maybe there's a roach trap in there...one of those roach hotels that they advertise on TV. Seems like a strange place for a roach trap though."

"It just doesn't make any sense. Roaches always go after something to eat, but I don't smell anything in there," said Shiloh as he stood near the forbidden locker. He couldn't help but visualize a fancy roach hotel with gourmet food and luxurious accommodations. He could even see roaches in tuxedos serving the other roaches. There had to be something interesting in there to attract those roaches.

"I want to grab one of them so we can take a closer look at it. There's something really odd goin' on in there. Maybe it's an unusual specimen," Desirae said. Evan was thinking how nice it was to have a girl around who seemed to be scientifically minded. Shiloh realized that Desirae was less bug-phobic than he was. She took out a small, plastic transparent box that she had found in the school's science class after band class was over.

Suddenly, the three of them stopped talking. They all heard a strange sound within the closed-off locker. It sounded like an alarm, but it was very muffled. "Is that what I think that is?" Shiloh asked.

"I don't know, but I think we'd better get out of here!" Evan said.

"Relax, it can't be dangerous because whatever it is, the school knows about it, since they closed off the locker," said Desirae.

"How do you know that they know about this?" asked Shiloh. He wasn't convinced that the principal or teachers had a clue.

"Wow...I never thought about that," said Desirae. "Maybe it's just a prank. Then again, we know at least the janitor knows something."

Just then another roach was moving in a quick-slow, quick-slow, zigzag pattern along the floor near the prohibited locker. The three friends watched in horror as it started to climb up to get inside the locker. Quick as a flash, Desirae grabbed it up gently in her right hand and deftly deposited it in the transparent box.

"I thought you hated roaches!" said Shiloh. He was stunned that she picked one up and handled it.

"If it means touching one of these to solve a mystery then I'll do it. I love mysteries. Besides, I pretended it was just a leaf to psyche myself out." Desirae explained.

Before they could examine Desirae's catch, they heard Ms. Sufferin coming down the hallway with her pointer. Desirae stashed the roach box in her pocket so Ms. Sufferin wouldn't see it.

"Can't you kids read?" asked Ms. Sufferin as she waved her fully-extended pointer at them. "Stay away from that locker!"

"Sorry, Ms. Sufferin, we were just leaving," said Shiloh. *So much for the teachers not knowing about the sealed-off locker*, he thought to himself.

"Oh, it's YOU again," she said, as she looked into Shiloh's face. Shiloh immediately cast his eyes down to avert her gaze, but he started to think about Desirae's dog-eat-dog picture and it took every ounce of his being not to break out in a laugh.

"What's in there?" asked Desirae as she tried to distract Ms. Sufferin from Shiloh so he wouldn't get into more trouble.

"None of your business," said Ms. Sufferin. "Don't the three of you have a class to go to?"

"Yes," said Evan. "We're leaving now. We had to get some stuff in our lockers."

The three students started to walk slowly away but when Shiloh turned around he noticed that Ms. Sufferin was already a distance away from them. She was talking to Janitor Tom who had just turned the corner from the adjacent hallway. She was waving her arms about as if she were upset, but Shiloh couldn't hear what she was saying. He noticed that Tom had his head down and was averting her gaze.

"We've got 10 more minutes. Let's go down to the lab," said Evan.

"What lab? Are you sure we have time?" asked Shiloh. "I don't want to be late for the next class. My next class is Phys Ed and there are usually penalties when you're late." Shiloh had once been late to PE class in fifth grade and had had to stay after school to clean muddy equipment as his punishment. He still hadn't forgotten that day. It hadn't been fun.

"Just follow me and hurry up," said Evan. Evan began to race down the hallway.

Desirae and Shiloh were a few steps behind. At the end of the hallway, there was a door that was labeled *Staff Only*, but Evan pushed the heavy door and proceeded down a winding metal staircase. His footsteps were making a lot of noise and Shiloh was worried that Sufferin or one of the other teachers would discover where they were, but no one seemed to be around.

Shiloh and Desirae followed Evan down into the bowels of the school. It was a dark cavern-like space and Shiloh was beginning to wonder what could possibly be down there. He was pretty sure they were all going to be late for class. He glanced at the clock on his phone. They had about 8 minutes left for recess and he needed at least 4 minutes to get to his other class.

"Where are we going, Evan?" asked Desirae. She was beginning to get worried about being late for her next class as well.

"We're here!" announced Evan as he pushed open an old, creaky door. When Desirae and Shiloh stepped inside they couldn't believe it. The room behind the door was old and dilapidated. It was about the size of a regular classroom, but it looked like an extension of Evan's bedroom. It was filled with large, ancient computers, computer parts, and an endless tangle of wires. Small, partially broken tech gadgets, including old, heavy cell phones, were set out on cheap, folding tables.

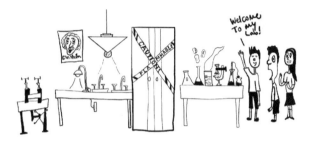

There were no windows so it was dark until Evan flipped the light switch and the room was filled with bright bluish light from incandescent commercial lamps. The lamps swayed gently from wires attached to the ceiling. There was a small printing press in one corner and in another corner, was a huge, steel industrial sink. Near the printing press was a large yellow cabinet that said "FLAMMABLE! CAUTION!" There was also one table that seemed to have biological specimens and flasks for chemistry work. The place had a chemical odor that smelled a little like vinegar.

"Wow! Cool! What is this place?" asked Desirae. She wasn't sure which area to check out first. It all looked fascinating. She did notice a large microscope on the biology table and had started to think about taking a closer look at the roach in the box.
 "It's my lab...my secret lab," said Evan.

"Secret? How could this place possibly be secret?" asked Shiloh.

"I thought that too, at least in the beginning," Evan said. "Remember when I was taking that botany class this past summer? They held the class here at Cornerstone and there weren't many students or teachers around. After class I started to come down here. At the beginning, I just set up one table, and when no one said anything I started to bring some more stuff."

"But what if somebody finds out?" Desirae asked.

"It's all old stuff that no one cares about. I dug up some of the school history and..."

said Evan, but Shiloh interrupted him before he went any further.

"Evan, according to my phone I have approximately three minutes to get to my next class. We'll talk history later. We've got to get going!" exclaimed Shiloh.

"Oh, no! I can't believe we're so late," said Desirae. "I've got tech class next and that's Sufferin's class."

"Let's meet down here at lunch," said Evan. "Then we can examine the roach and think about ways to find out what's in the locker without making the teachers or anyone else suspicious."

Just then, the bell rang announcing the start of the next class session.

"Meet down here at noon!" said Evan. "I'll send you both a text if I can get back to the locker earlier." They all raced upstairs and sped down the hallway in separate directions.

Luckily, when Shiloh reached his Phys Ed class several other students were late so he wasn't singled out. The coach, Mr. Robertson, didn't seem upset. After all it was their first day at Cornerstone so he cut them some slack.

Shiloh was a natural athlete so he wasn't worried about Phys Ed. He could do it all in his sleep and it was a good thing too because his mind was occupied with thoughts of the mysterious locker and Evan's amazing secret lab.

Evan's next class was science and his teacher, Mrs. Engelstrom, was so nearsighted that she didn't even notice he was late. Within the first few minutes she asked a science question about the ratio of dark matter to dark energy in the universe. Just for fun she put up all the answers on the board. They were all wildly off target except for Evan's. His answer was correct and that was the exact moment that he became Mrs. Engelstrom's pet.

Desirae was the only one who suffered from their lateness to class. She tried to be inconspicuous as she slid into Ms. Sufferin's classroom, but unfortunately Ms. Sufferin recognized her from the hallway conversation at the locker. She was given an old PC to work on instead of one of the newer computers. The other students didn't notice, but Desirae had a high-speed computer at home and the old piece of junk she was using in Sufferin's class was ready for Evan's spare parts table in the secret lab. She was bummed, but class passed by quickly enough. She was able to get through Ms. Sufferin's assignment in half the time of the other students and she quietly researched common types of roaches and their habits while Ms. Sufferin was busy with another student. She couldn't wait until lunchtime so they could go down to Evan's lab again.

Chapter 4
The two troublemakers

11:00 am to 12:00 pm

At the end of PE class, Shiloh got another
text from Evan on his phone:

```
It is now 11:00 am.
Desirae & I will meet
you at your locker at
11:03 am. Be there.
We have a plan.
```

Shiloh wrote back:

```
Will get there ASAP.
Will have to sprint from
PE class.
```

He'd been thinking of nothing else but the
mysterious locker, but unlike Evan he
hadn't really thought about what they
could do to discover its contents. His
friend seemed to enjoy challenges the
way most people would enjoy eating a
sandwich, bite by bite. Thinking of
sandwiches had made Shiloh hungry. It
was still an entire hour before lunch
break and all the running around in PE
class had given him an appetite.

As soon as the bell rang, he headed out of class in the direction of the lockers. He couldn't remember what his next class was so he fished inside his backpack for his orientation packet. He kept moving in the direction of the lockers as he opened up his packet. His next class was technology and he groaned when he saw "Ms. Sufferin" as the designated instructor. After the problem, he'd had with Sufferin throughout the day, he knew that he'd better get to her class on time.

He quickened his pace when he saw that Evan and Desirae were already there. He almost didn't see Max run up alongside of him.

"Hey, where you headin'?" asked Max.

"Going to tech class," said Shiloh. He didn't really want Max to notice that they were at the locker so he deliberately slowed down his pace. He was afraid that Max would talk too loudly and attract attention.

"That's where I'm headin'," said Max. "Did you get your paper done for Mr. Thomas's class tomorrow?"

"I thought we had a couple of days to work on it," said Shiloh. He was beginning to wonder whether he had missed something Mr. Thomas had said.

"Yeah, but it doesn't hurt to turn things in early. Teachers like that. They think it's because you're into their subject. Mine's done already," said Max.

"Done? What? How could you...?" Shiloh asked.

"I've got my sources," said Max as he smirked. "See you in class."

Shiloh was relieved when Max took a turn off the locker hallway into Sufferin's class. Now he could talk to Desirae and Evan without Max interfering. As he walked up, he noticed that Desirae had put on some shiny pink lip gloss. He liked the way it made her lips so shiny. Apparently, Evan did to, because he couldn't stop staring at her lips. The three of them stood together, but before they could say anything they heard the muffled sound of a cuckoo clock.

"Is that coming from...?" Desirae asked.

"Yep," said Evan. He had used C-E-G-I-F-A to open up Shiloh's locker. He had borrowed a toy stethoscope from Mrs. Engelstrom's class and had it on the wall of Shiloh's locker next to the sealed-off locker.

"I can hear something ticking, but it doesn't really sound like a clock," said Evan.

"What could it be? I'm so curious. Maybe we should try picking the lock," said Desirae.

"What if we pick the lock and there's an alarm that goes off?" Shiloh asked. He was getting worried that the three of them were going to get in trouble.

"I say let's try it, but not now, we don't have time. We should all try to get here when class is in session so no one will be wandering the halls," said Evan. "Let's each get a bathroom pass around 11:40 and meet here. Then, if we pick the lock and an alarm goes off we can run and no one will see us."

"I can't do it," said Shiloh. "I have tech class next and Sufferin will be watching me like a hawk. I keep having run-ins with her."

"I think I can get a hall pass from Mrs. Engelstrom. I have her science class next," said Desirae. "I can meet you here."

"I have PE class. I'll just claim vertigo or something and get out early," said Evan. "You can meet us at lunch, Shiloh."

"Verti what?" asked Desirae.

"It's like dizziness but the room looks like it's spinning," answered Evan.

"Then why wouldn't you just say dizziness? It's more believable," Desirae questioned as she flipped her hair over her shoulder and rolled her eyes.

"What do you mean, it's not believable?" asked Evan.

"Do you really think the PE teacher is going to believe that you know what vertigo is? He'll know right away that you're making it up," said Desirae.

"Look guys, we don't have time for arguing," Shiloh said gruffly.

He was a little annoyed that Evan didn't have some glorious plan for him to escape from tech class. Then it occurred to him that Evan might want some time alone with Desirae.

"Are you sure you can't get out of class somehow?" Desirae asked as she twirled her hair and smiled at Shiloh.

Shiloh was about to say he would try, but when he saw Evan's face he decided not to. He had been right that Evan wanted to be alone with Desirae. "You guys go ahead without me. I'll meet you at lunch down in the lab. I've gotta go. I'm gonna be late again. Sufferin is going to hit me with that pointer!"

Shiloh sprinted to Ms. Sufferin's class and slid into the seat next to Max's. Luckily, Mr. Thomas was talking to Ms. Sufferin outside class and she seemed focused on every word he was saying.

"Where were you?" asked Max in a rough-sounding whisper.

"Stopped to say hi to some friends from my old school," said Shiloh. He didn't like lying to Max, but it wasn't a total lie, since Evan was a friend from elementary. He just didn't want Max to know what they were up to.

"Hey, look at that!" said Max. "It looks like Ms. Sufferin is flirting with Mr. Thomas."

Max was right. Ms. Sufferin was laughing at everything that Mr. Thomas was saying although they were too far away for Max and Shiloh to hear their conversation. Unfortunately for her, it looked like all the flirting was going one direction. Shiloh hoped that the Sufferin-Thomas conversation would put Ms. Sufferin into a better mood than she usually seemed to be in. He thought Mr. Thomas was way too nice for Ms. Sufferin, but his mom was always saying that "opposites attract."

Shiloh saw Mr. Thomas finally break away from Ms. Sufferin so she had to start teaching her class. For a second it looked like she seemed to be in a better mood, but Shiloh could see her face gradually morph from her hideous smile into a scowl. She walked over to her desk and grabbed the pointer. The class immediately got very quiet. Evidently, her reputation had traveled fast. Nobody wanted to mess with her.

"Today, I want all of you to take out your orientation packets. You will be working in pairs today, so if I have any trouble out of you it will be double the punishment!" Her gaze traveled to Shiloh.

She continued, "Your goal for this project is to organize your schedule on the Google calendar so that it will be available for you to view in the cloud both at home or at school or on your phones, which I still don't understand why you need to have."

The class snickered at that. Ms. Sufferin slammed her pointer on the desk. "QUIET!" You could hear a pin drop after her outburst.

"When you're finished, your partner will check your work against the information in your packet. Make sure you allow for the appropriate travel times you'll need between classes. We've been lenient today, but that's only because it's the first day. For the rest of the week there will be penalties for being late," said Ms. Sufferin as she looked pointedly at Shiloh.

Great, Shiloh thought to himself. *Now I'm going to have trouble with her all year.*

Max passed Shiloh a note under the table. Shiloh opened it in his lap, but he kept his eyes fixed on Ms. Sufferin so she wouldn't see. The note read:

```
Lenient? Ya right!
What's your number so I
can text you?
```

Max had scrawled his cell phone number on the note too.

Instead, of writing Max a note, Shiloh sent him a text so they didn't have to use paper notes anymore.

```
If she thinks she's
lenient then she
probably thinks Navy
Seal training is like
going to Disneyland.
```

Unfortunately, Max forgot to put his phone on silent and the ding was as loud as a fire alarm in the classroom. Ms. Sufferin's head jerked so fast that it looked like it was about to twist off. She took two large steps with her pencil-thin legs and she was right at his side. She grabbed his cell phone.

"Did I make a joke? What's this?" she asked as Max turned beet red. She whacked her pointer down hard on the top of Max's desk. "Who sent you this text?" She said only a few inches from his face.

Max was stumbling over himself to speak. The words just wouldn't come out. He nodded in Shiloh's direction. *Uh-oh* Shiloh began squirming in his seat.

"You again! You're a regular comedian, aren't you?" she said. "Well, we'll see how funny it is when you have to give up your phone too." She walked back to her desk and put the pointer and Max's phone down. Shiloh quickly sent one more short text to Evan:

> ```
> Don't text me. Cell in
> enemy hands.
> Secret lab @ lunch.
> ```

Ms. Sufferin made Shiloh walk up to her desk to deposit his phone. She also partnered him with Max so she could keep an eye on "the two troublemakers."

Once they got started on the project, Shiloh found that although Max was rough around the edges he was good with technology. They made quick work of scheduling their classes in Google calendar. They even figured out how to get the prompts on their phones although they couldn't test it to see if it was working.

In the meantime, Desirae and Evan had managed to get their hall passes and were back at the mysterious locker. Evan was attempting to pick the lock with a fully extended wire paper clip. He had jammed it into one of the holes where the lock's shackle attached to the rest of the lock and was twisting it around.

"I have to wait for it to make a clicking sound according to the YouTube video," Evan quietly said to Desirae in his best scientific voice. "I've never tried to pick one before. If this doesn't work, I'll try the pressure and turning method."

Desirae was standing behind him when she heard wheels rolling. It was Janitor Tom. He was starting to turn the corner into the locker hallway. Desirae whispered close to Evan's ear, "Stop. Tom's coming."

Chapter 5
Darwin

12:00 pm to 1:00 pm (lunch)

"Hey, I told you kids to get away from there," Janitor Tom said as he rolled up with his bucket and mop.

"Don't you ever stop mopping?" asked Desirae. She stepped in his direction and turned so he would have to face her to answer her question with his back to Evan.

"I wish I could," Tom said, his voice dripping with resentment. "But you kids are the messiest, sloppiest..." He went on and on without noticing that Desirae had managed to successfully distract him from what Evan was doing.

Thankfully, Desirae had given Evan sufficient warning. He had stashed the paper clip in his pocket and leaned against the locker casually hoping to make it look like they were just chatting in front of it, while he also secretly prayed that no roach would slip out and start crawling on him.

Evan's hand was a little sweaty from trying to pick the lock, but that wasn't the only reason. He was so nervous around Desirae, and all he could think about was the fruity scent of her beautiful hair. He wished she would be his girlfriend, but he had already noticed that she seemed to like Shiloh better than him. But he wouldn't give up just yet, he was hopeful that their joint love of science might help his cause. He had noticed that she had seemed impressed with his secret lab.

"Sorry," mumbled Evan to Tom.

Tom looked up as if surprised that Evan was there. He was so caught up in his rant that he forgot why he had even started talking to the miscreants

"You should be sorry." Tom said. "Why don't you tell me what you're sorry for." He tried to get it out of them, hoping to jog his memory.

Desirae and Evan looked at each other in confusion. "Ummm...we were...trying to....actually all we were doing was talking and you came and started yelling at us." Desirae folded her arms and plastered a look of innocence on her face.

"You sure about that?" asked Tom. He looked puzzled. "Ok then, but you kids get outta here. Get to class."

Evan and Desirae turned to walk away. Tom took his mop and bucket and went down the hall shaking his head. They waited until they were out of Tom's sight to head down to the secret lab.

They were just about to get to the entrance of the lab when Evan got this text from Shiloh:

```
On my way. Got my cell
back. Going to pick up
food to bring. You want
anything?
```

Desirae was looking over Evan's shoulder when he got Shiloh's message. "I'm starving," she said. "Tell him I'll eat anything but egg salad."

Evan wrote back:

```
Yes, thanks. We'll pay
you back. Anything
except egg
salad.
```

Shiloh was lucky that at the end of tech class Mr. Thomas came back to talk with

Ms. Sufferin, which Shiloh thought was weird. He couldn't possibly be into Ms. Sufferin could he? That thought was so repulsive he got rid of it quickly.

Fortunately for Shiloh, Ms. Sufferin was so distracted that when he asked for his cell phone back she gave it to him without taking her eyes off Mr. Thomas. He had no idea where the lunchroom was but there was a delicious smell of pizza wafting from one of the hallways so he just followed his nose.

The first thing he saw when he got there was his sister Shasha. She was "holding court" with a group of her friends. His older sister was in 7th grade and she was even more popular than Shiloh. Shiloh paused for a few minutes to talk with her. All her friends stopped their chatter as Shasha introduced him as her "little brother." Shiloh heard the girl next to Shasha say, "This is your *little* brother? He's cute." It was kind of weird to hear an older girl say that he was cute and Shiloh's face turned a little flush.

"Shasha, can I talk to you for a sec?" Shiloh asked her.

"Sure," she said as she kept eating her piece of pizza. She was picking the pineapple off of it and stacking it in a neat pile.

"No, I mean...privately," he said.

"Oh, yeah," said Shasha. She turned to her friends. "I'll be right back."

"Sorry. Can I borrow some cash? I need to buy a couple of sandwiches for some friends so I can take them down to the secret lab," Shiloh said. He hated to ask Shasha for money because she never let him forget it. "I'll pay you back tonight."

"Sure, sure. As I recall, you still owe me from the last time you borrowed money from me. Wait, what? Secret lab? What are you talking about?" she said as she pulled out some cash from her pocket. "Are you feeling okay? You look weird."

"Yeah, I guess so. It's just that everything's been weird today. There's this mysterious locker that's sealed off. Evan, and Desirae, this girl we just met, and I can't figure out what's in it, but these roaches keep crawling in there," Shiloh said breathlessly.

"Ew, I hate roaches," said Shasha. "Not a good topic at lunch."

"Sorry," said Shiloh. "We keep hearing strange sounds in there too, like muffled alarms and cuckoo clock sounds."

"I think you're going cuckoo," said Shasha. "Do the teachers know about the locker?"

"Yeah, Ms. Sufferin and Tom, the janitor, keep trying to get us away from it," said Shiloh. "Look...I gotta go. I'm supposed to meet Evan and Desirae down in the secret lab. Evan's got an entire space to himself down in the basement. The teachers don't even know about it."

"What? Now I know you're really going off the deep end. That isn't possible," she said as she put her hand up to his forehead. "Are you sure you don't have a fever? How is Ms. Sufferin this year? She still wearing ugly clothes and waving around her stick?"

"Yup," said Shiloh. "Long pointer, gray clothes, still there."

"Oh, yeah. She's a bundle of joy. I had her for tech class last year. I'm so glad to be in 7th grade this year," she said. "The teachers get better as you go higher up."

"I'll tell you more at home tonight," said Shiloh as he grabbed the cash that Shasha handed him and went to buy enough lunch tickets. Shasha gave him an odd look as she went back to her friends who were giggling at the lunch table. He wanted to take pizza back to the lab, but it would be too difficult to carry so he grabbed three tuna sandwiches, some packages of chips, some sodas, and some chocolate chip cookies. The lady at the lunch counter stared at him.

"You eatin' all this yourself?" she asked.

"No, it's for me and my friends," Shiloh said. "Is that okay?"

"Your secret's safe with me, honey," she said as long as you have the tickets to pay for all of it. "I guess I better give you a paper bag, huh?"

Shiloh grabbed the stocked-up paper bag and started to run in the direction of the secret lab. Then, he realized he should slow down so he wouldn't call attention to himself.

He walked fast and looked at his cell phone here and there just so he would have a second to come up with an answer if someone stopped him. Luckily, most of the kids and teachers were in the lunchroom so he was able to wind his way down to the lab without being seen.

When he got there, Evan and Desirae were examining the roach that she had captured earlier in the day under the microscope. Shiloh was so hungry, but his stomach turned slightly at the thought of it. Desirae had had the foresight to pop some air holes in the transparent box in which it was captured so it wouldn't die. However, the box wasn't large so it wasn't moving much. She had placed the box with the roach in it on the microscope's stage.

"Nothing unusual about this specimen. It's a male *Periplaneta americana*," said Desirae, "commonly known as the American cockroach."

"I almost expected to see some kind of electronic device on it," said Shiloh.

For a second, Evan stared into space, then he screamed, "Shiloh, you're a genius! That's it! Turn it over, Desirae."

The three of them hovered above the microscope. Desirae was the first to look through and she couldn't believe what she saw. There was a small chip attached to the underside of the roach. The color blended in so perfectly that it was difficult to see.

"WHAT IS THAT?" she exclaimed.

"Let me see," said Evan. When Evan got up to the microscope, both Desirae and Shiloh were quiet. As he kept his eye fixed on the roach's underside, he grabbed a pencil and paper and started jotting down some quick notes. Then, Evan moved away from the microscope slowly and sat down on a stool.

"Evan, what is it?" asked Shiloh. He had never seen Evan with this facial expression before. He looked as if he had discovered some deep, dark scientific secret.

"It's a Global Positioning System chip," said Evan. "Someone is tracking every move these roaches make."

"What?" said Desirae. "Why on Earth would somebody want to know where these roaches are going?" Desirae took the roach off the microscope's stage. She didn't want him to get overheated. She was starting to think of him as a pet.

"Well," said Evan. "We know a few facts. We know that there are several roaches. Let's assume that they all have these GPS chips. We also know that they seem attracted to the forbidden locker. We've heard some noises from there that sound like clocks. We know that the teacher and the janitors don't want us to mess with the locker."

"Maybe they don't all have those GPS chips. Maybe it's a coincidence and this is the only bionic roach," said Shiloh.

"Yes, he's special. He's more evolved than an ordinary roach. I think I'll call him Darwin," said Desirae.

That made Shiloh laugh. "I can't believe you're naming a roach, Desirae."

"Why not?" said Desirae. "I don't mind roaches. In some countries, they have certain species as pets, you know."

"Darwin is the perfect name for him," said Evan. "He had some beetles and termites named after him. Of course, those were the scientific names."

"I think we should stop talking about Darwin the roach now and eat our sandwiches," said Shiloh. "I've been starving for two hours!"

Evan cleared some tech gadgets off one of the folding tables so they could have their indoor picnic. They unwrapped their sandwiches and started to eat. Shiloh could see that Evan was deep in thought as he strategized their next move. He wondered if Desirae could help cure his mom from her bug phobia.

Evan drank a swig of his soda and then he said, "I think someone is controlling how Darwin moves."

Chapter 6
Escaping the drama

1:00 pm to 2:00 pm

By the time it was the beginning of the next class period, the three friends had their plan in place. Their next class was drama and happily they had all been assigned to Mrs. Whitlock's class. Shiloh was surprised that Evan had selected drama as one of his electives since he was usually shy when he had to present in front of the class.

Before lunch was over, they had decided that between classes they would try two more strategies to find out what was in the locker. For Strategy 1, Evan wanted to try out a mini x-ray machine that he had been tinkering with in the lab. It was his own creation and he had never tested it yet.

Desirae had performed a delicate operation on Darwin as part of Strategy 2. She had removed his chip with a pair of tweezers and attached a small camera that Evan made to him instead. The camera was wireless and if it worked properly it would transmit a video to

Desirae's cell phone as Darwin was roaming around inside the locker. Shiloh couldn't believe that she had managed to get Darwin to hold still. Shiloh wondered if the bionic roach could somehow sense that he was part of an important mission. The thought made him smile.

They needed time to try out their new strategies, but since they were all in the same class, it seemed unlikely that they would be able to come up with an excuse for a hall pass. They decided to play that by ear once they got a feeling for Mrs. Whitlock since they hadn't met her yet.

When they got to Mrs. Whitlock's class they were surprised by what they saw. Mrs. Whitlock was wrapped in a dress that seemed like multi-colored scarves sewn together in a haphazard way. Her hair was wiry strands of black with a huge streak of white in the front. She had on purple lipstick and her fingernails were quite long with matching purple nail polish. She spoke in a deep, dramatic voice that resonated throughout the class.

Shiloh was thinking that she could have read the phone book and made it sound interesting. But Mrs. Whitlock's appearance wasn't the only thing that was unusual about drama class. The room was a hodgepodge of scenery and costumes. There were chairs for the students, but no desks. Mrs. Whitlock didn't care if the chairs were lined up in neat rows. As a result, the room was a complete mess, but somehow it seemed to be just the right environment for drama class. And Mrs. Whitlock was beyond wonderful. She immediately got the students involved by explaining to them that their first project was to get together in groups of four and write a short 10-minute skit. Then, in the next two classes, they would perform their finished skits.

Before they began, Shiloh raised his hand to ask a question. "Do you care what topic we pick for our skit?"

"What's your name, young man?" Mrs. Whitlock asked.

"Shiloh, ma'am," he said.

"I have three characteristics for every successful skit," she replied. "One, it must be wildly creative. Two, it must have interesting characters. And three it must have fascinating dialog. Beyond that, it can be about any topic you like as long as it's legal and moral. Does that answer your question?"

"Yes!" said Shiloh, "Can we choose our own team?"

"You may for today, but in the future, I reserve the right to group you differently once I find out your dramatic strengths and weaknesses," she said.

Desirae glanced over at Shiloh and smiled. Evan was worried about what his own dramatic weaknesses might be. He was thinking that his crush on Desirae might end up being a dramatic weakness. She wasn't paying any attention to him at all. Her eyes were riveted on Shiloh.

The three friends picked up their chairs and moved them into a semicircle so they could come up with an idea for their skit. Desirae still had Darwin stashed in her shirt pocket. At lunchtime, she had given him a few crumbs of her sandwich to eat. He seemed to like the leftover flakes of tuna. They had started to settle in and kick around some ideas when another student approached them.

"Can I join you guys?" she asked. She seemed shy and uncomfortable. "Sorry to butt in, but your team is the only one with three instead of four. My name's Roxy."

Desirae was the first one to speak up. "Sure. The more the merrier. Pull up a chair."

Roxy had a heavy backpack with her and instead of slinging it on her back, she was holding it in her right hand and trying to drag the chair with her left hand at the same time. She was moving around like a ragdoll with her arms and legs in different directions with her wavy hair falling over her face. Shiloh got up and took the chair from her and moved it quickly into their semicircle so that the chairs were arranged with Desirae at the left and Evan, Roxy, and Shiloh, in that order, to Desirae's right.

Evan introduced himself and then introduced Desirae and Shiloh. Roxy seemed overly happy to be allowed into the group. It made Shiloh think of when he and his family had first moved to their city when he was in second grade and how awkward he felt.

"Did your family just move here?" Shiloh asked.

"Yes! How did you know that?" Roxy replied. She gave Shiloh a smile, which annoyed Desirae.

"Just a lucky guess," he said. "You'll like it once you settle in."

"OK, let's see," said Evan. "We need it to have interesting characters, and smart dialog. It's going to be hard to do all of that in 50 minutes."

"I think I have an idea that might work," said Desirae, "that is, if Roxy doesn't mind."

"Why would I mind?" asked Roxy.

"Because you'd be the main character. You'd be the new girl in school," said Desirae.

"You want to do a skit on how it is to be the new girl?" said Roxy.

"I don't think that's interesting enough," said Evan. "We need some conflict."

"How about if we show me wandering around begging groups to let me in and how you guys were nice enough to include me. It was all pretty dramatic in my thoughts!" Roxy said as she made swirling motions with both of her hands and pointed to her forehead.

"Okay with me," said Evan. "I'll be the friendly one who welcomes you." Evan was hoping that playing up to Roxy would make Desirae notice him more.

"So that leaves me to be the mean girl who casts you out," said Desirae. "I can be pretty convincing as mean but don't worry, I don't really mean it, Roxy!"

"Ha ha....don't worry!" exclaimed Roxy. "I won't think you really mean it!"

Desirae responded with a smile that didn't quite reach her eyes. She muttered, "If you only knew."

"Did you say something?" Roxy asked.

"Me? No. I didn't say anything. Carry on," Desirae said quickly. Relieved that Roxy seemed to believe her.

They were all writing pieces of the dialog and passing it to each other for review. About 20 minutes in, Shiloh took his phone and sent a text message to Evan and Desirae.

```
I like Roxy. I think we
should tell her about
the locker and see if we
can head out of class
early to try Strategies
1 and 2.
```

Desirae texted back to Shiloh and Evan:

```
I'm not sure yet. Let's
wait until we know her
better.
```

Shiloh texted back to Evan and Desirae:

        She might be able to
        help us.

Desirae texted back:

        Alright, go ahead and
        ask her to help. Maybe
        it won't be so bad to
        have another girl on
        this team!

Plus, I'll keep an eye on her, Desirae
thought. She asked Shiloh to switch places
with her so she could push her chair
closer to Roxy's. There was so much noise
going on in the classroom that no one
noticed that Desirae was talking to Roxy
for a solid 10 minutes. After all, the story
was complicated. At points, Evan and
Shiloh noticed that Roxy had a confused
look on her face. It wasn't clear whether
the story Desirae was telling her didn't
make sense or whether Roxy wasn't
confident that Desirae was telling her the
truth. At the end, she seemed convinced
that Desirae wasn't lying. Then, Desirae
gave her some instructions and Roxy
nodded her head.

It all happened so fast that Evan and
Shiloh didn't realize what was going on
until it was over. Desirae took the

transparent box, clicked it open, and dumped Darwin on the floor. She was worried about him, but she was confident his survival instincts would kick in and he would head back to the forbidden locker.

Roxy jumped up on her chair and screamed, "Look!!! It's a huge roach! Gross! Get it! Get it!"

Evidently, Mrs. Whitlock was just as bug phobic as Shiloh's mom. She jumped up on her chair as well and thrust her arms upward with her scarf-like dress billowing in the breeze above her knees. Some kids got up and ran after Darwin, but most of them just tucked their legs under them or stood on their chairs. As confusion mounted, Desirae, Evan, and Shiloh escaped and soon afterwards Roxy followed.

Desirae was right about Darwin. He climbed up on the edge of a piece of scenery, opened his wings wide, and glided from Mrs. Whitlock's class out into the hallway where the lockers were. Then, he ran tightly along the edge where the floor met the wall.

When Desirae, Evan, and Shiloh got to the sealed-off locker, they had about 10 minutes to spare. Evan tried Strategy 1 right away. The mini x-ray machine gave them a picture of the inside, but it was so dark that they couldn't easily make out what they were seeing. They could see that there was some type of machinery, but its size, form, and parts remained a mystery.

Roxy got there by the time they were ready to start Strategy 2, but Darwin was nowhere in sight. "How did I do?" she asked breathlessly.

"I think you could win an academy award!" said Desirae. She thought maybe Roxy wasn't so bad after all.

"Thanks, Desirae!" Roxy said. She was flush from running and from receiving Desirae's praise.

"Ya you did amazing!" Shiloh said, appreciatively.

I wouldn't say amazing, thought Desirae. *On second thought, maybe Roxy needed to–*

"Look! There's Darwin!" exclaimed Evan, interrupting Desirae's thoughts.

"Are you sure it's him? Maybe it's another roach," said Shiloh.

Desirae ran to Darwin and picked him up. "He's fine! It must be him. The camera's still on!" She made a bridge from her hand to the slit under the locker door and Darwin ran right in.

"How far away does the wireless camera work, Evan?" asked Shiloh.

"About 300 feet. It's a good thing too because it's time to move on to the next class," said Evan.

Chapter 7
A mystery solved while another begins

2:00 pm to 3:00 pm

It had been a long, but exciting, first day at Cornerstone Middle School. Shiloh couldn't wait to get home and tell Shasha and his parents everything that had happened. He wondered if they would believe him. The last class period was their homework session. Shiloh was hoping to spend part of the time working on Mr. Thomas's assignment since his Google schedule showed that he would have math class on Tuesdays and Thursdays. Math class almost always had a lot of homework.

At Cornerstone, teachers got together to supervise the homework session. It took place in the large open auditorium and students were allowed to sit where they wanted. The teachers roamed around and were available to answer questions if the students needed their help. They also kept an eye on students to ensure they were actually using the time to study and not just goof off.

Desirae quickly found them a section where the four of them could sit together. The auditorium seats had flip-down tables, just like the food tables in an airplane, so the students had desktop surfaces to place their laptops, phones, or old-fashioned notepads to work. As soon as they sat down they tuned in to Darwin's live video feed to see where he was in the locker.

The leftover crumbs from Desirae's tuna sandwich at lunch must have given Darwin a boost of energy. He was zooming all over the locker and the four of them were crowding their heads as close together as possible so they could see what was happening. So far, all they could piece together was some sort of machinery and a bunch of tangled wires. They also saw other roach heads and antennas as Darwin crawled over other roaches in a pile. Evidently Darwin had some friends with him.

"Yuck," said Roxy. "I don't want to be around when you open up that locker."

"Yeah, I wonder how many of those roaches are still alive," said Shiloh.

"Double yuck," said Roxy.

"We've got to get out of here early and get that locker open," said Desirae. "I don't think I'll be able to sleep tonight unless I know what's in there. Besides I need to take Darwin out of there and bring him home with me."

"How will you be able to tell which one is Darwin if we open the locker?" asked Evan.

"I'll be able to pinpoint his location by the video feed once we get closer," said Desirae.

"I can't believe you're thinking of keeping him as a pet," said Roxy as she laughed. "I think it's amazing that he survived Mrs. Whitlock's class after all that screaming and kids running after him."

"Roaches are definitely survivors. Did you know they can survive a nuclear explosion!" exclaimed Evan. "Isn't that amazing?"

"What's amazing is that you know that without checking the internet," said Shiloh as he laughed.

"What does he know without checking the internet?" asked Max as he came up to

Shiloh. Shiloh was sitting on the end of the aisle.

"Lots of stuff," said Shiloh. He introduced Max to everyone, but as he turned to his left where the others were sitting he gave them a look as if to say *don't tell him anything.*

"Hey, you gonna introduce me?" Max asked Shiloh as he eyed Desirae.

"Gang, this is Max, Max this is Evan, Roxy and Desirae," said Shiloh, "we're working on a skit we need to finish for drama class." Shiloh didn't totally trust Max and didn't want him to know about the mysterious locker.

"You want some help?" Max said as he stared at Desirae who blushed with embarrassment and flattery. "I could help you with that...for a price."

"Thanks, I think we're good," said Shiloh. "See you later." He was hoping that Max would take the hint and go find a seat somewhere else in the auditorium. He saw that Evan was starting to look mad at Max and Desirae making googly eyes at each other.

"Alright, catch you guys later," he winked at Desirae before he sauntered off.

Desirae and Roxy started giggling after Max was a distance away, which made Evan even more annoyed.

Just then Mr. Thomas came on stage. "Students, I have an announcement to make. Can I have a few minutes of silence please?"

The sounds went from loud and boisterous to quiet and muffled in just a few seconds.

As soon as it got quiet, Mr. Thomas continued, "We have an important visitor at the school today. This is Mr. Joseph Hamilton, he is a researcher who wants to talk to you about the importance of STEM programs. Without further ado, I'll be giving him the floor. Please give him your undivided attention."

Mr. Hamilton walked out on stage. He was a tall, middle-aged man with dark hair that had streaks of gray in it. His skin was tan and he looked elegant in his three-piece suit.

Desirae started to feel a weird sensation in the pit of her stomach. She knew she's seen Mr. Hamilton before she just couldn't remember where or when.

Shiloh and Evan were both feeling odd too.

"Hello students, I appreciate that the principal and faculty at Cornerstone Middle School have given me the opportunity to speak to you today. STEM stands for science, technology, engineering, and math. We want more students to be interested in STEM programs because there are so many things you can do. Do any of you ever wonder how gum gets a flavor or how you can make different paint colors? Maybe you wondered how the military makes those really fast planes or how you access the internet. My specialty is in technology." There was a small hum of noise from the students at this point in his speech. Mr. Hamilton paused and then he smiled slightly as he continued, "Do any of you know what a spy is?"

Mr. Hamilton continued to talk about technology and surveillance and how many satellites were over the earth. As soon as Mr. Hamilton got off stage, the noise level in the auditorium increased.

"Mr. Hamilton looked so familiar to me," said Desirae. "I think I've seen him somewhere before."

"I thought that too," said Shiloh.

"Me too," said Evan.

"I don't recognize him," said Roxy. "Maybe he just looks similar to someone you know."

It was hard for the four of them to settle down and work on the skit together, but they did and by the time the bell rang, they were finished with it.

"We're going back to the sealed-up locker, Roxy. Do you want to go with us?" asked Desirae.

"Nope. I have no interest in seeing those yucky roaches. I'll catch you guys in the next drama class. Have a good one," Roxy said as she waved goodbye.

"Bye Roxy," said Shiloh.

"See you tomorrow," said Evan. He watched Roxy as she left and hoped that Desirae would notice, but Desirae and Shiloh were already making a dash for the locker and Evan had to hurry to catch up to them.

They got there before too many students were around. Most of the students had taken their backpacks into the auditorium since it was the last class period.

"Okay, guys, cover for me. I'm going to try to pick the lock again," said Evan. He took the extended paper clip out of his pocket and inserted it into the hole where the shackle attached to the lock. This time he got lucky and there was a clicking sound. He quickly snapped the lock open. As he flung the door open, the red tape ripped. Some of the roaches inside flew out while others started running down the outside of the locker. It had happened too quickly to see which one was Darwin. There was a huge tangle of wires and a ticking device.

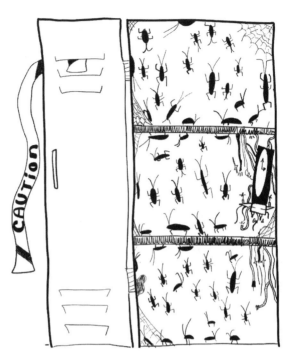

"What have we done? We shouldn't have opened the door! What were we thinking?" said Desirae.

"Don't worry, Desirae. I can't believe this, but it's pieces of a failed science project that I wanted to enter into last year's science competition. I was never able to finish it," said Evan.

"How did it get here?" asked Shiloh.

"I have absolutely no idea," said Evan. "Last time I saw it, it was in my closet at home under a pile of stuff. I was close to finishing it, but the last time I tinkered with it, I still couldn't get it to work. I wonder if my parents know about this."

"What was it supposed to do?" asked Desirae. She was fascinated by the fact that Evan had tried something so ambitious. He was thrilled when he saw the expression of admiration on her face.

"It had a tracking device inside it and it was supposed to work with mini drones outdoors. I forgot that I programmed all those different crazy sounds. The sounds were signals for the commands given to the drones by remote control. It's essentially a spying device," said Evan, "but, of course, it was supposed to be used to keep properties safe."

"Wow! The roaches were actually being controlled by your device! Somebody has gotten your invention to work. It's just being used for indoor spying instead of outdoor spying," said Shiloh.

"Maybe they were eventually going to attach cameras to the roaches like we did with Darwin," said Desirae. "The roaches would be good spies. They can squeeze in anywhere."

Just then they heard a sound. It was a janitor coming down the hallway. He had a bucket and a mop. They expected to see Tom but it was someone else.

"That's it!" exclaimed Desirae. "Now I know where I saw Mr. Hamilton before. He was Janitor Tom."

"No way!" exclaimed Evan. "Are you sure?"

"Let's check," said Shiloh. "I took a snapshot of him with my phone earlier in the day. I thought it was suspicious because he kept mopping down the same hallway. Maybe it was Mr. Hamilton and he was disguised so he could do the security testing without anyone noticing."

The three friends looked closely at the photo. Desirae was right. Mr. Hamilton and Janitor Tom were either the same person or identical twins.

The mysterious locker had been opened, but it was only a portal to many more mysteries to come.

Acknowledgments

I want to thank my family for their unflagging support and love during this time where I doubted myself. This book was conceived to entertain children across the world and give them a glimpse into the Onyx world.

Special thanks to:

Shiloh: Without your input and affirmation I would not know whether I hit the right note with kids.

Shasha: Thank you for your tireless encouragement when I wondered if I could do this.

Shalom: Thank you for the comical illustrations and inspiring the character of "Tom" through your hilarious performance on Onyx Kids.

Sinead: Thank you for the cover and the absurd "Ms. Sufferin" embodied by your performance on Onyx Kids.

Mirthell: My love, thank you for always believing in me and supporting me even when it meant self-sacrifice. I love you.

I love you all.

About the Author

Rita Onyx is a member of the Onyx Family who also include Shasha, Shiloh, Shalom, Sinead, and Mirthell. Together they have a successful social media and YouTube following with over 1 million subscribers and over 1 billion views across their channels. Check out Onyx Family, Onyx Kids, Onyx Life, Playonyx, and Cardionyx on YouTube, Prime Video, Facebook, Instagram, Twitter, and Amazon to find their new videos, books, and merchandise.

Other Onyx Kids Books:

Getting to Know Onyx Kids

Visit Onyx Kids online at
www.onyxkids.com for more fun!

Made in the USA
San Bernardino, CA
31 March 2020